15.95
6/10/02

Sixteen Miles to Spring

WRITTEN BY **Andrew Pelletier**

ILLUSTRATED BY **Katya Krenina**

ALBERT WHITMAN & COMPANY
MORTON GROVE, ILLINOIS

To Erin. And the whole Pelletier mob—
Mom and Dad, Steve, Mark, Matt, Dan, John, Joe, Mary, and Christine—
endless source of inspiration, support, and humor. — A. P.

To little Elliott, born September 11, 2001.
May there always be Spring and Peace in your world. — K. K.

Library of Congress Cataloging-in-Publication Data

Pelletier, Andrew Thomas.
Sixteen miles to spring / by Andrew Thomas Pelletier; illustrated by Katya Krenina.
p. cm.
Summary: When Maddy and her father go for a drive, they meet two unusual
men and witness the magical change of seasons from winter to spring.
ISBN 0-8075-7388-4 (hardcover)
[1. Spring — Fiction.] I. Krenina, Katya, ill. II. Title. PZ7.P3639 Si 2002 [E] — dc21   2001004317

The design is by Scott Piehl.

For more information about Albert Whitman and Company,
visit our web site at www.albertwhitman.com.

WE ALL KNOW THAT SPRING is the season between winter and summer, when the world wakes up from its snowy sleep and the days begin to grow longer and warmer. But what causes the seasons?

As the earth spins around the sun, it tilts on its axis, an imaginary line drawn from the North to the South Pole. This tilt affects how much sunshine hits our part of the earth at different times of the year. In winter, the top half of the earth, the Northern Hemisphere, is tilted away from the sun. The sunshine that does reach us is indirect and weak. As a result, winter nights are long, and the weather is cool. At the same time, the other half of the world, the Southern Hemisphere, is tilted toward the sun, and it is summer there.

But as the earth continues its journey around the sun, this situation begins to reverse itself. Beginning nearest the equator, the imaginary line where the two hemispheres meet, the Northern Hemisphere gradually sees more sunshine.

The days get longer, and spring begins to march slowly northward. The official first day of spring is March 20 or 21, when the sun is above the equator and days and nights are of equal length.

Spring can roll toward us at a rate of sixteen miles a day, as in this story, but of course this depends on many conditions — how deep the snow is, how strong the wind, whether it is cloudy or clear. Some years it seems as if spring will never arrive at all.

Yet it always does.

Be patient, and watch for the signs: the sun becoming just a little bit warmer, the icicles under the eaves dripping, dripping . . .

One day, almost without warning, a patch of earth will appear, and a brave crocus will poke its head up to take a look around. Then, as the sun grows still stronger, and daylight lingers later and later, the first robins will arrive, and more flowers and songbirds. And before you know it, it really, *truly* will be spring!

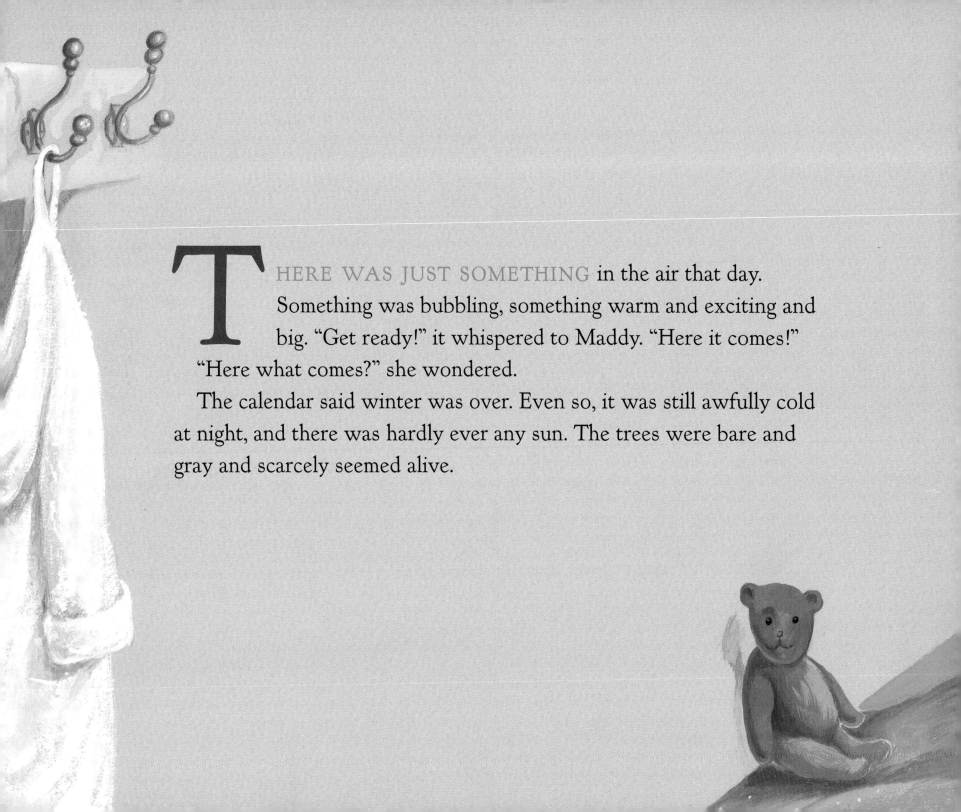

THERE WAS JUST SOMETHING in the air that day.
Something was bubbling, something warm and exciting and
big. "Get ready!" it whispered to Maddy. "Here it comes!"
"Here what comes?" she wondered.

The calendar said winter was over. Even so, it was still awfully cold
at night, and there was hardly ever any sun. The trees were bare and
gray and scarcely seemed alive.

Out on the porch, Maddy found Dad staring across the brown, dull lawn, over the patches of snow and down toward the road. He, too, was sniffing the morning. "Hey, Maddy-girl," he said. "What do you say we drive into town and see what's new at the garden store?"

"Okay!" Maddy smiled. It was fun going out with Dad.

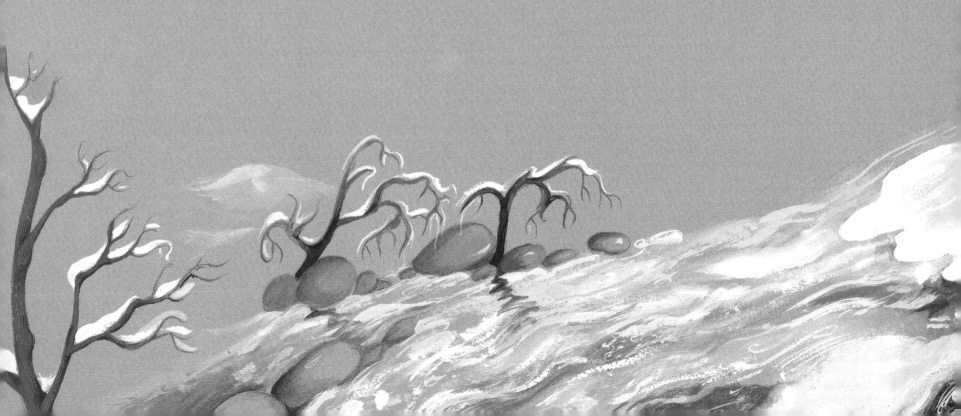

They climbed into the car and turned out onto the dirt road, big
gobs of mud splashing up behind. As they rumbled across the wooden
bridge, Maddy could see brown water rushing below, carrying away
all the melting ice and snow. Only a week before she could have
walked right across the frozen brook. *Something* sure was happening.

Suddenly Dad pulled over. "Will you get a load of that jalopy?" he said. An old-fashioned pickup truck was putt-putt-putting ever so slowly along the road. It was painted emerald green, and it was piled high with boxes and bags and tools and junk, all poking out this way and that. The truck itself was clean as a whistle.

The jalopy sputtered to a stop beside them. Maddy noticed some shiny letters painted on its side: *Sixteen Miles to Spring*. "I wonder what that means?" she asked herself.

Two men climbed out. One was very tall and very skinny. He wore a big straw hat and bright green overalls. The other man was short and round and bald and dressed in yellow from head to toe. The two had the brightest smiles Maddy had ever seen.

Dad and Maddy got out of the car. "Hiya, gents," said Dad. "Looks like you've broken down. Can we give you a hand?"

"Broken down?" replied the tall skinny one, in a high squeaky voice. "No, old Janey here never breaks down!"

"We're just waiting for something," said the short round one, in a big deep voice. He pulled out a gold pocket watch that sparkled like the sun. "Should be along any minute now!"

"My name's Wilbur," the short man said. "And that stringbean there is Wiley." Both men bowed and shook hands with Maddy and Dad.

"I'm Maddy," said Maddy. Suddenly she was bursting with questions. "Where do you come from? Where are you headed? Why do you call your truck 'Janey?'"

"Slow down!" said Wilbur, with a laugh. "One at a time!"

"Where do we come from?" repeated Wiley. "Why, from down south a ways! Where the sun always shines and the beaches are fine and the oranges and lemons are quite divine!"

"And Janey? Why, Janey's just her name, just like yours is Maddy," said Wilbur. "A truck has to have a name, you know!"

"How does Janey stay so shiny?" Maddy asked.

"Janey takes a shower every day!" said Wilbur, grinning.

"Whether she needs one or not!" added Wiley. He removed his hat, and a cloud of butterflies appeared from underneath and began flying all around them.

"Why, where did those critters come from?" asked Wilbur. For some reason, this made them both laugh so hard that their faces turned blue.

"What does 'sixteen miles to spring' mean?" asked Maddy, once they had finally stopped laughing.

"Why, sixteen miles is as far as we drive each day," said Wiley. "No more, no less. We start way down south, you see, not long after Christmas. A few weeks from now we'll be as far north as we can go and flowers will grow!"

"That way spring's always waiting for us, just around the corner!" said Wilbur. A fat robin flew up and sat down atop his bald head, but he didn't seem to care.

Suddenly Wiley held up his finger and cocked his head, listening. "Here she comes!" he said.

Wilbur checked his golden watch. "Right on time!" he added with a nod.
The breeze started to blow harder. The air grew warmer and warmer.

A raindrop hit Maddy smack on the chin. Another one splattered in her ear. By now the wind was whooshing past, like a train charging down the track. "Hold onto your hats, folks!" yelled Wilbur.

It began raining so hard that a river ran down Maddy's neck. Her boots were filled right up to the brim. The rain felt nice and warm, sort of like taking a shower, and Maddy really didn't mind.

"Maybe we could use your help after all!" called Wiley. He rummaged in the truck and hauled out a big burlap sack. "Quick!" he said. "Grab a handful!"

Maddy reached inside the sack and pulled out a handful of stuff that looked like straw and seeds and dirt, mixed up with sparkly specks of green and gold and every other color under the sun. Dad and Wilbur and Wiley each grabbed a handful, too.

"Get ready!" cried Wiley. "Set . . ."

"Now!" Wilbur shouted. At that they all threw their handfuls of seedy stuff high into the swishing, blustery sky.

As fast as they had come, the wind and rain passed on up the road. The sun burst out from behind the clouds. Maddy took off her jacket and let the sun shine on her skin and dry her hair. She hadn't felt this warm and cheerful in a long time. She felt like dancing! When she turned to look at Dad, he and Wilbur and Wiley were hopping around in the middle of the road, stomping in the puddles and yodeling at the sky like a bunch of fools. Before Maddy quite knew what was happening, she was hopping and stomping and yodeling, too!

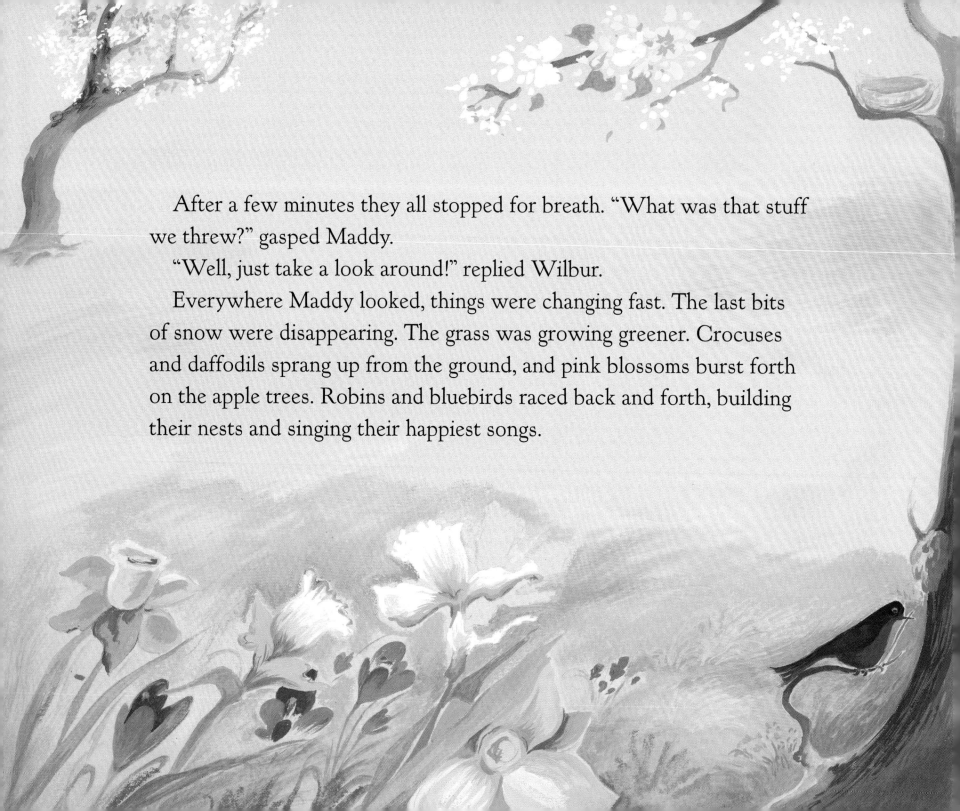

After a few minutes they all stopped for breath. "What was that stuff we threw?" gasped Maddy.

"Well, just take a look around!" replied Wilbur.

Everywhere Maddy looked, things were changing fast. The last bits of snow were disappearing. The grass was growing greener. Crocuses and daffodils sprang up from the ground, and pink blossoms burst forth on the apple trees. Robins and bluebirds raced back and forth, building their nests and singing their happiest songs.

Suddenly Maddy knew what it was she had been feeling that morning, what it was she had smelled on the breeze. It was the smell of fresh dirt and new leaves and every sort of growing thing.

It was spring.

Just then a large flock of geese passed over them, heading north and honking loudly. Wilbur and Wiley flapped their arms and honked right back. "We'd better get going!" said Wiley. "We don't want things to get ahead of us!"

As the two men hopped back into the truck, Wilbur called to Maddy. "If you want to help again tomorrow, why, you know where to find us!"

"I sure do!" answered Maddy, pointing up the road.
"It's just sixteen miles to spring!"